Lily
the Rain Forest
Fairy

Special thanks to Narinder Dhami

ISBN 978-0-545-60528-1

Previously published as Green Fairies #5: *Lily the Rainforest Fairy*
by Orchard U.K. in 2009.

All rights reserved. Published by Scholastic Inc., 557 Broadway, New
York, NY 10012, by arrangement with Rainbow Magic Limited.

12 11 10 9 8 7 6 5 4 3 2 1   14 15 16 17 18 19/0

Printed in the U.S.A.   40

This edition first printing, July 2014

Lily
the Rain Forest Fairy

by Daisy Meadows

SCHOLASTIC INC.

Jack Frost's
Ice Castle

Rainspell Island

Wildlife
Garden

Lake

Vacation Cottage

Harbor

Beach

Coral
Reef

Ice Cap

The Earth Fairies must be dreaming
If they think they can escape my scheming.
My goblins are by far the greenest,
And I am definitely the meanest.

Seven fairies out to save the earth?
This very idea fills me with mirth!
I'm sure the world has had enough
Of fairy magic and all that stuff.

So I'm going to steal the fairies' wands
And send them into human lands.
The fairies will think all is lost,
Defeated again—by me, Jack Frost!

Contents

Food From the Forest

"Look, Kirsty," Rachel Walker called as she hurried through the trees. "I think I found some wild onions!"

"Oh, great!" Kirsty Tate, Rachel's best friend, ran to join her, swinging her basket. The two girls were on a nature walk in the forest near their vacation cottage on Rainspell Island, where they were spending the school break with their families.

Rachel and Kirsty knelt down and gazed at the onion plants. They had long, thin leaves and greenish-white flowers. The girls knew that not so far underground there were onion bulbs.

"The Junior Naturalist class we went to this morning was fun, wasn't it, Kirsty?" Rachel said with a smile. "I never realized there were so many things growing wild on Rainspell Island that you can eat. Do you have the soup recipe the teacher gave us?"

Kirsty took a leaflet labeled MUSHROOM SOUP out of her basket.

"Remember, Jo told us that we should only take as much as we need," Kirsty reminded Rachel. "Otherwise the plant won't be able to reseed itself, and then there won't be new onion plants next year."

Rachel checked the recipe ingredients. Then she carefully pulled some of the onion bulbs from the ground and put them in Kirsty's basket. The girls had already collected some sprigs of sweet-smelling wild thyme and other herbs.

"Now we just have to find some mushrooms, and we can make soup for dinner tonight!" Rachel jumped to her feet. "We have to remember to check the booklet about mushrooms that Jo gave us, because we need to make sure the ones we find aren't poisonous."

"Isn't it amazing how many different plants and animals there are in the forest?" Kirsty remarked as they wandered along the path again.

"I know," Rachel agreed. "It was so

interesting this morning when Jo
explained how all the plants and animals
and birds rely on one another, and on
the forest, for their food and shelter."

Kirsty glanced around. The
leaves on the trees were
turning red, gold, and
yellow, and
squirrels were
busily leaping
around,
collecting
nuts to store
for the winter.
"I love
Rainspell,"
Kirsty said happily. "I'm so glad
we came back." Rachel nodded
in agreement.

Rainspell Island was really special to Rachel and Kirsty because it was where they first became friends, *and* where they first met the fairies!

No one else knew about Rachel and Kirsty's magical friendship with the fairies. In the past, King Oberon and Queen Titania had often asked for the girls' help whenever they had problems with Jack Frost and his goblins. But this time, it had been Rachel and Kirsty's turn to ask the fairies for *their* help.

The girls had been shocked when they returned to Rainspell Island to find litter on the beautiful golden beach, so they'd used their special lockets to visit Fairyland and ask the king and queen to help clean up the human world.

The king and queen had named seven fairies-in-training the Earth Fairies for a trial period. If they completed their allotted tasks, their special jobs would become permanent. Rachel and Kirsty had been thrilled to find out that these fairies would work to make the world a cleaner, greener place. But they knew that humans had to help, too.

But just as the Earth Fairies were about to be presented with their new wands, Jack Frost and his goblins had zoomed in on an ice bolt. The goblins had grabbed the wands, and then Jack Frost's icy spell had sent them spinning away into the

human world. Jack Frost was trying to prevent humans from becoming greener, but Rachel and Kirsty were determined to find the wands and return them to their rightful owners. The Earth Fairies needed to start their important work!

"I wonder if we'll find another wand today," Kirsty remarked as the girls made their way through the woods.

"Remember what Queen Titania always says," Rachel replied. "We have to wait for the magic to come to *us*! But four of the wands are safely back in Fairyland now, at least."

"And we know that fairy magic can't fix *all* our environmental problems," Kirsty added. "We humans have to do everything we can to help as well!" She pointed at a tree ahead of them. "Look,

Rachel, isn't that a silver birch?"

"Yes," Rachel agreed, admiring the
tree's beautiful silvery
trunk.

"Jo showed us one this
morning. And look,"
she went on, "there
are some wild
flowers growing at
the foot of it."

As the girls were
looking at the tiny
purple flowers,
Kirsty felt a drop
of rain splash
onto her
face.

Suddenly, more rain began to pour down on them from the darkening sky.

"Quick, Kirsty!" Rachel called to her friend. "We can take shelter under that cluster of trees over there."

The girls ran toward the trees and huddled underneath them.

"That's better!" Kirsty said, shaking her damp hair out of her eyes. "The rain's really coming down now, Rachel."

Rachel was about to reply when suddenly she cried out in delight.

"This is amazing!" She pointed down at the grass at her feet, where there was a circle of gleaming white mushrooms.

"Fantastic!" Kirsty laughed. "Isn't it lucky that we came here to find shelter?" She opened the leaflet their  teacher had given them, and checked the pictures carefully. "I think these mushrooms are safe to eat, but we'll ask

our moms, too," Kirsty said at last.
"They'll be wonderful in our soup! I'll
gather as many as we need, and no more
than that."

Kirsty bent down to pick a few
mushrooms. But then she gasped with
surprise.

There, hidden under one of the
mushrooms, was Lily the Rain Forest
Fairy!

Amazing Rain Forest

As Rachel bent to look, Lily fluttered
out from under the mushroom. She
wore green wide-legged pants, and an
off-the-shoulder green top. Her long
black braids flew out behind her as she
hovered in front of Rachel and Kirsty.

"Girls, I'm so happy to see you!" Lily announced joyfully, turning a cartwheel in the air. "I'm on the trail of my wand, and there's no time to lose. Rain forests everywhere need my help!"

"Do you know where your wand is, Lily?" asked Rachel eagerly.

"Is it close by?" Kirsty added.

Lily's face fell a little. "My wand isn't on Rainspell Island," she replied. "It's far away, in a rain forest!"

Rachel and Kirsty looked disappointed.

"As you know, girls, I only have a little fairy magic without my wand," Lily went on. "I have just enough to take the three of us to the rain forest, but unless I find my wand, I may not have enough magic to bring us home again!" She looked solemnly at Rachel and Kirsty. "I'll understand if you don't want to take the risk and come  with me."

"We'll come," Rachel said, a determined look on her face. Kirsty nodded in agreement.

After all their many adventures with the fairies, the

girls were confident that they'd be able to help Lily outwit the goblins and get her wand back! They also knew that time stood still in the human world while they were in Fairyland or on a special fairy mission.

Lily looked relieved. "Thank you, girls," she said. "We'll go right away."

Their hearts thumping with excitement, Rachel and Kirsty linked hands as Lily snapped her fingers. Immediately, a faint mist of glittering fairy dust floated down around the girls. They shrank down to fairy-size, and soft, fluttery fairy wings appeared on their backs.

Then Kirsty and Rachel noticed that the raindrops still

falling from the sky were beginning to sparkle and shimmer. Soon the raindrops became so bright and dazzling that the girls had to close their eyes. The next moment they felt themselves flying through the air.

"Welcome to the rain forest, girls!" Lily announced with a laugh.

Rachel and Kirsty could feel the heat on their skin before they even opened their eyes. When they did look around, both girls gasped in utter amazement.

The three fairies were hovering among the treetops of the rain forest, high above the ground. The trees were growing so close together, their branches intertwined to form a thick, leafy canopy. Hot, dazzling sunshine shone here

and there through the gaps. Long ropes
of vines hung from the trees, swaying
lazily in the slight breeze. The air was
warm and damp, and all the leaves,
exotic flowers, and ripe fruits
were wet with drops of
moisture that made their
colors glisten. Rachel and
Kirsty could see bananas,
coconuts, and mangoes
growing near them. They
could also hear the noisy
songs of tropical birds,
as well as the calls
of animals hidden
among the trees.
"This is the most amazing
place I've ever seen!" Rachel
murmured, her eyes wide.

"And the hottest place I've ever been!" added Kirsty, as the three friends fluttered down to the rain forest floor.

Lily smiled. "The rain forest is *very* hot and wet," she explained. "It gets lots of sunshine and rain every day, and that's why it looks so green and beautiful." She pointed up at the canopy of overlapping branches and leaves above them. "You might be surprised to know that most of the plant and animal life in the rain forest is up there in the canopy, not down on the ground."

"Really?" Rachel began, but then she gave a gasp of surprise as a golden-colored monkey suddenly jumped out from the middle of a tree near her. Chattering to himself, the monkey began to swing through the rain forest from branch to branch. Meanwhile, Kirsty had spotted a bright green frog with large red eyes sitting on a nearby leaf. As Kirsty watched, the frog hopped away.

"The animals that live in the canopy have different

ways of getting around," Lily explained. "They fly, they hop, they jump, and they swing from branch to branch! Come and have a closer look."

Rachel and Kirsty followed Lily as she zoomed up to the treetops, zipping neatly among the interwoven branches. The girls saw lots of birds, insects, flowers, and fruit in the canopy that were strange and unfamiliar. There was so much to see, they hardly knew where to look next!

"The rain forest is very important because it provides a home for many different kinds of plants and animals," Lily explained. "It's also very important for humans, because the trees help to produce the planet's oxygen."

"This is fantastic!" Kirsty sighed happily as a beautiful red-and-blue dragonfly fluttered past. "But we can't forget that we came here to look for your wand."

"You're right," Lily agreed. "And I can sense that my wand is around here *somewhere*. We'll start searching for it right away."

But at that moment, Rachel thought

she heard a noise above the cries of the birds and animals. She frowned. Had she *really* heard something, or had she just imagined it?

"What's the matter, Rachel?" asked Kirsty.

"I thought I just heard something kind of weird," Rachel replied. "Can you and Lily hear it?"

Kirsty and Lily listened hard, but at first they couldn't hear anything unusual. Then, all of a sudden, a loud noise echoed through the canopy.

A creature was screeching anxiously at the top of its voice!

Goblins in Bulldozers

Rachel, Kirsty, and Lily were horrified by the distressed call.

"The sound is coming from over there." Kirsty pointed to a thick clump of trees. "I think we should go and see who it is!"

"Good idea," Rachel replied, and the three friends flew toward the trees.

"Let's split up and take a look around," Lily suggested in a low voice. "It'll be faster that way. But be careful, girls!"

Kirsty fluttered up higher to search the canopy while Rachel and Lily began looking among the trees down below.

Suddenly, Lily cried out. "Girls, over here!"

Kirsty and Rachel zoomed over to her. Lily pulled them behind a large leaf so they were out of sight. She then pointed to the next tree. A big scarlet-and-blue parrot sat on a branch, squawking loudly.

"I wonder what he's saying," Rachel whispered.

"Let's go and ask him!" Lily replied.

Kirsty, Lily, and Rachel flew toward the parrot. The bird looked surprised when they landed on the branch next to him. It screeched again.

"A little magic will help us understand what he's saying," said Lily. She snapped her fingers and a few glittery sparkles drifted around the parrot.

"Hello, I'm Lily the Rain Forest Fairy," Lily went on. "And these are my friends, Kirsty and Rachel. What are you trying to tell us?"

The parrot fluffed out his bright

feathers, looking very upset. "Green hurts trees!" he said.

Lily, Kirsty, and Rachel looked bewildered.

"Help save trees!" the parrot screeched, flapping his wings frantically.

Lily shook her head, baffled. "I'm afraid I don't understand what you're trying to tell us. Can you *show* us what you mean instead?" she asked.

The parrot nodded. Instantly, he spread his wings and zoomed away through the trees.

"Quick!" Lily gasped. "Or we'll lose him!"

The three friends dashed after the parrot as fast as their wings could carry them. They ducked and dived between branches and leaves, occasionally

coming face-to-face with surprised birds
and monkeys.

"There he is!" yelled Rachel, catching a
glimpse of scarlet and blue ahead of them.

Lily, Rachel, and Kirsty rushed toward
the parrot. Luckily, he was slowing
down so they could
catch up with him
a little.

"Look, he
stopped in that
clearing,"
Kirsty said.
She could see
the parrot
perched on
the branch of
a tree.

"But what's

that terrible noise?" Rachel asked.

Lily and the girls flew closer. To their amazement, they saw five big bulldozers roaring around the clearing. The bulldozers were knocking into one another and banging into the trees. As Kirsty, Rachel, and Lily watched, one of the smallest trees was hit particularly hard by one of the bulldozers and toppled over. There were shrieks and cries of fear as panic-stricken birds flew out of the branches, and monkeys swung to safety in nearby trees.

"This is terrible!" Kirsty exclaimed. "We have to stop them!"

Rachel glanced at the bulldozer drivers, who were wearing hard hats. She looked more closely and pointy spotted green ears and noses peeking out from under the hats.

"The drivers are goblins!" Rachel gasped.

Then Kirsty noticed something else. One of the goblins was holding a stick, and every time another bulldozer got too close, the goblin leaned out of his cab and poked the other driver with it. As he did so, the stick shimmered in a faint cloud of fairy dust.

"That goblin has Lily's wand!" Kirsty exclaimed.

Fruit Storm

"Now I understand why the parrot kept saying 'Green hurts trees,'" Lily exclaimed. "My rain forests are in danger because humans are chopping down the trees—and now the goblins are destroying them, too!"

"We need to stop them, *and* get the wand back!" Rachel said anxiously.

The three friends zoomed into the clearing, keeping high above the bulldozers. They flew over to the parrot, who was still sitting on a branch, his wings drooping miserably.

"We're going to do everything we can to stop the goblins. We won't let them destroy the rain forest," Lily told him. "Why don't you go home, where you'll be safe?"

"Thank you," the parrot squawked, and he flew away.

"STOP!" Kirsty yelled as one of the bulldozers

crashed into the tree the parrot had been sitting in.

"They can't hear us over the noise of the engines," said Rachel. "Let's fly down lower."

Quickly, Lily and the girls darted toward the bulldozer of the goblin holding the wand.

"Stop!" Rachel shouted, as they hovered around the driver's cab. "What are you doing?" The goblin looked up at them and scowled. "Playing bumper cars, of course!" he retorted, sticking his tongue out at them. He reversed his vehicle and rammed into a tree with a jolt, before racing toward one of the other bulldozers.

Lily and the girls dashed after him.

"Please give my wand back!" Lily shouted at the goblin as she, Rachel and Kirsty landed on the window of his cab. "I need its magic to look after rain forests all over the world, and to help all the creatures that live in them!"

Before the goblin could say anything, two other goblins in bulldozers rumbled straight toward him. The three bulldozers all crashed into one another,

and the impact sent the three fairies
tumbling off the window. They hurtled
through the air, but landed safely on a
large, soft leaf.

"Girls, are you OK?"
Lily asked.

"We're fine,"
panted Kirsty,
"but we have
to get the
goblins off these
bulldozers!"

Lily nodded. "They're disrupting
the rain forest ecosystem," she said with
concern. "That means they're putting all
the plants, animals, and trees in danger."

"Let's fly up to the canopy," Rachel
suggested. "It'll be quieter, and maybe
we can come up with a plan."

Lily and the girls fluttered higher, and landed on a tree with large green and yellow fruits clustered near the top of the trunk. The goblins were still charging around in the bulldozers and whooping gleefully whenever they hit a tree or one another.

"What can we do?" Lily asked sadly. "I don't have enough magic to stop them."

Rachel and Kirsty looked around for something that might help.

"But all I can see are leaves, flowers,

and fruit," Rachel said to herself. She stared at the fruits hanging around them. She didn't know what they were, but she could see that the young fruits were green, while the ripe ones were bright yellow. Some of them were rotting on the branches. Rachel pushed one and it fell to the ground, just missing the nearest bulldozer.

"Oh!" Rachel gasped out loud. "I think I have an idea. Kirsty, Lily, follow me!"

Rachel zoomed off through the canopy. Puzzled, Kirsty and Lily flew after her. But they soon realized what Rachel was up to when they saw her gently knocking down the big ripe, rotten fruits onto the goblins below them. The fruit landed on the bulldozers, splattering their windshields with pulp and seeds.

"Great idea, Rachel!" Kirsty said as she and Lily started knocking the fruit down, too. "If the goblins can't see, they'll have to stop!"

As fruit rained down on the bulldozers,

the goblins shrieked with annoyance and
drew to a halt. They all turned on their
windshield wipers, and began clearing
the mess away so they could see. Rachel,
Kirsty, and Lily tried desperately to
knock down more and more fruit, but it
was very difficult to do it quickly
because they were so small.

"This isn't working!" Rachel
exclaimed in dismay, shaking her head.
"We'll have to try something else."

Meanwhile, the goblins had cleared
their windshields and were revving up
their engines again. Clouds of black
smoke belched from their exhaust pipes.
As Kirsty watched, her face suddenly lit
up.

"Now *I* have an idea!" she announced.

Animal
Army

"Maybe we can still use fruit to stop the bulldozers," Kirsty said.

"But we know that won't work." Rachel sighed.

Kirsty grinned. "We can use the fruit in a *different* way," she replied, and she pointed to a bunch of bananas down below them. "We can stuff it in the bulldozers' exhaust pipes! I saw it work in a movie once."

"Are you sure?" Rachel asked. "That sounds kind of dangerous."

"But we've got to stop those bulldozers," said Lily thoughtfully. "How about we take out the bananas as soon as the bulldozers' engines stop? Then we can make sure no permanent damage is done."

Lily and the girls flew down to the clearing, keeping far away from the

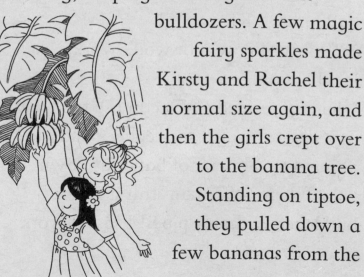

bulldozers. A few magic fairy sparkles made Kirsty and Rachel their normal size again, and then the girls crept over to the banana tree. Standing on tiptoe, they pulled down a few bananas from the big clump hanging on the tree.

Quickly, Lily zoomed over to the bulldozers. She flew around trying to distract the goblins, who all stopped the bulldozer engines to swat at the fairy.

Meanwhile, Rachel and Kirsty crept into the clearing. They both went about putting bananas into the bulldozers' exhaust pipes. When Lily saw that the girls had blocked all the pipes, she flew high into the canopy. The goblins immediately turned the bulldozers'

engines back on, and the machines began to move slowly forward again.

But the bulldozers had hardly moved at all before they started sputtering and choking to a halt. The goblins looked puzzled.

"What's going on?" the goblin with the wand roared, hopping down from his cab. "My bumper car stopped!" Suddenly, he spotted Rachel and Kirsty darting across the clearing. "Those girls are interfering again!" the goblin shouted angrily.

The other goblins jumped down from their bulldozers, and they all charged at

Rachel and Kirsty. But Lily was quicker.
She dashed toward the girls and snapped
her fingers. Immediately, Rachel and
Kirsty shrank down to
fairy-size, and the
three of them flew
up into the air
out of the goblins'
reach. Lily
waved her arms
again and the
bananas magically
popped out of
the bulldozers' exhaust pipes.

"We don't know what kind of trouble
the goblins will cause with my magic
wand!" said Lily. "We shouldn't get too
close to them."

"Give us the wand back, please!"

Rachel called to the goblins below. "It belongs to Lily, not you."

The goblin with the wand chuckled. "Catch me if you can!" he taunted. He jumped up onto his bulldozer, grabbed one of the long vines hanging from a tree, and swung away through the rain forest. The other goblins did the same.

"They're getting away!" Kirsty cried in dismay, as the goblins swung speedily from vine to vine.

"After them!" Lily yelled.

The three friends gave chase. The goblin with the wand glanced over his shoulder and saw Rachel coming up fast behind him. Grinning, he gave the wand to the goblin swinging past him, like a runner in a relay race. Rachel made a desperate grab for the wand, but the second goblin immediately handed it to a third, who quickly swung away from her.

"Keep your eye on the wand, girls!" Lily called, as the third goblin passed it neatly back to the first goblin.

It didn't take the goblins long to get the hang of swinging on the vines, and soon they were moving along incredibly fast. Rachel, Kirsty, and Lily did their best to fly faster themselves, while also trying to keep track of the wand. But it was very difficult, because the five goblins passed it back and forth so often.

"We need help!" Lily panted as the goblins pulled far ahead of them. She

snapped her fingers, and Rachel and
Kirsty saw some fairy sparkles dancing
in the air.

A few moments later, the girls heard
rustling noises in the leaves behind them.
Glancing over their shoulders, they
were amazed to see a whole army of
animals and birds appear. There were
orangutans and other different kinds of
apes and monkeys.
There were
macaws and
toucans and lots
of brightly
colored birds,
as well as
lizards,
snakes,
and insects.

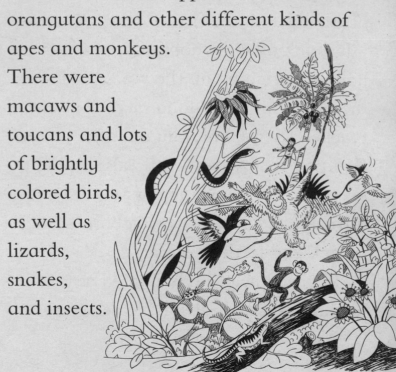

Right at the front was the scarlet-and-blue parrot Lily and the girls had met earlier.

"Thank you for coming, everyone," Lily said gratefully. "We have to catch those goblins and get my wand back!"

Chattering and cooing, whistling and chirping, the animals and birds of the rain forest swung, jumped, hopped, wriggled, and flew after the goblins.

"They're much faster than we are!" Rachel laughed, as the animal army easily sped ahead of the fairies.

"But how will they stop the goblins?" Kirsty wondered. Then her eyes widened as she watched the goblins swinging from vine to vine. "Oh! Maybe we could use the *vines* to trap them!"

All Tied Up

Lily nodded. She zoomed over to the parrot and whispered something to him. The parrot then squawked something to the array of animals.

Rachel and Kirsty watched as the parrot led the other animals and birds after the goblins. They grabbed long ropes of vines in their teeth, beaks, or paws on the way. Some went in one direction, some in another, and some of

them even managed to get in front of the
goblins. Soon they had the goblins
surrounded on all sides.

"*Now!*" Lily called.

At once the animals swooped forward
while still holding the vines. They
trapped the goblins.

"Hey!" the goblin with the
wand shouted furiously as
the animals and birds
began neatly
wrapping the
vines around
them. "What's
going on?"

In just a few
moments, all the
goblins were
tightly bundled up

like a vine-wrapped package. They
yelled and struggled, but they were tied
too tightly to get free.

"Nice work, everyone!" Lily laughed.

Rachel and Kirsty flew
over and took the wand
from the goblin, who
glared at them. They
carried it to Lily, and
the instant the fairy
touched it, the wand
shrank to match its
rightful owner's size.
Rachel and Kirsty
grinned at each other.

"Now, you've caused
enough trouble for today!"
Lily said, pointing her wand at the
goblins. A stream of fairy dust shot

toward them, and the vines that held them prisoner untied themselves. "It's time you went home to Jack Frost's castle."

Grumbling bitterly, the goblins swung themselves through the trees and out of sight.

I

Lily turned to
the girls. "Thank
you for being brave
enough to come
with me," she
said, smiling.
"Now that I have
my wand, I can send you safely home.
But first, I must get rid of those horrible
bulldozers!"

The friends hurried back to the
clearing. Lily quickly waved her wand
and used her magic to heal the damaged
trees and stand them upright again.
Then, with a shower of magic dust, she
reduced the huge machines to fairy-size.
"At least the loggers who own these
bulldozers won't be able to do any more
harm for a while," she said.

"I need to get back to Fairyland, girls," Lily said, "and I will tell everyone there how wonderful you've been today! I couldn't have reclaimed my wand without you. Now I can begin my work of protecting the rain forests — and there's so much to do!"

"I wish we could do more to help." Kirsty sighed. "The rain forests are so beautiful, but they're also so far away from where we live."

"You can help by telling other people about the rain forests," Lily suggested. "Let them

know more trees are being cut down
every day, and that *we* have to stop it."

"We will," promised Rachel.

Lily smiled and pointed her wand at
the girls. "Good-bye!" she
called as a stream of
fairy sparkles lifted
Rachel and Kirsty
off their feet
and whirled
them into
the air.

In the blink of an eye, Rachel and Kirsty found themselves back in the forest on Rainspell Island. The rain had stopped now, and the sun was peeking through the clouds.

"It's not as warm as the rain forest!" Kirsty laughed, kneeling down to place the mushrooms in her basket. "Wasn't that a *fantastic* fairy adventure, Rachel?"

Rachel nodded. "And, like Lily said, we can tell everyone all about the trees in the rain forest being destroyed." She thought for a moment. "Maybe we could get in touch with a school in one of the rain forest countries, like Brazil, and start a tree-sponsoring program?"

"Oh, that's a great idea," Kirsty exclaimed, picking up her basket. "And we could organize some fund-raising events at our schools. We could have one where everyone dresses up as rain forest animals!"

Rachel laughed. "There are lots of things we can do," she said, "but right now our mission is to make these mushrooms into a delicious soup!"

Rachel and Kirsty found Nicole, Isabella, Edie,
Coral, and Lily's missing magic wands.
Now it's time for them to help

Milly
the River Fairy!

Join their next adventure
in this special sneak peek. . . .

A Fairy Afloat

"It's definitely colder than yesterday,"
Rachel Walker said, as she and her best
friend, Kirsty Tate, strolled through
Rainspell Park. "I can't believe we were
so warm on the beach at the start of the
week—and today we're all wrapped up
in our cozy sweaters!"

Kirsty grinned at Rachel. "And *I* can't

believe we were swimming in the ocean with Coral the Reef Fairy a few days ago," she said in a low voice. "Imagine how freezing cold the water must be right now!"

Rachel shivered at the thought. "She'd have to use a *lot* of fairy magic to keep us warm today, wouldn't she?"

The two girls smiled at each other as they walked through the park. It was fall break, and they were both here on Rainspell Island for a week with their parents. Rainspell Island was the place where Kirsty and Rachel had first met. They'd shared a very special summer together . . . and now this vacation was turning out to be every bit as magical!

"Oh, I love being friends with the fairies," Kirsty said happily, thinking about all the exciting adventures they'd had so far. "We really are the luckiest girls in the world, Rachel."

"Definitely," Rachel agreed. Golden-brown leaves tumbled from the trees every time the wind blew, and Rachel noticed just then that some of the trees were already bare. "Well, it's definitely windy enough today to sail our boats," she said as a yellow oak leaf floated down and landed at her feet. She glanced at the paper boat she was holding. Both girls had made one back at their cottage that morning. "They're going to speed along with this breeze behind them."

"Here's the lake now," Kirsty said as they rounded a corner and saw the stretch of blue water ahead of them. . . .

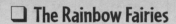

RAINBOW magic™

Which Magical Fairies Have You Met?

- ☐ The Rainbow Fairies
- ☐ The Weather Fairies
- ☐ The Jewel Fairies
- ☐ The Pet Fairies
- ☐ The Dance Fairies
- ☐ The Music Fairies
- ☐ The Sports Fairies
- ☐ The Party Fairies
- ☐ The Ocean Fairies
- ☐ The Night Fairies
- ☐ The Magical Animal Fairies
- ☐ The Princess Fairies
- ☐ The Superstar Fairies
- ☐ The Fashion Fairies
- ☐ The Sugar & Spice Fairies

SCHOLASTIC

HIT entertainment

Find all of your favorite fairy friends at
scholastic.com/rainbowmagic

RMFAI

RAINBOW magic™

SPECIAL EDITION

Which Magical Fairies Have You Met?

3 stories in each one!

- ☐ Joy the Summer Vacation Fairy
- ☐ Holly the Christmas Fairy
- ☐ Kylie the Carnival Fairy
- ☐ Stella the Star Fairy
- ☐ Shannon the Ocean Fairy
- ☐ Trixie the Halloween Fairy
- ☐ Gabriella the Snow Kingdom Fairy
- ☐ Juliet the Valentine Fairy
- ☐ Mia the Bridesmaid Fairy
- ☐ Flora the Dress-Up Fairy
- ☐ Paige the Christmas Play Fairy
- ☐ Emma the Easter Fairy
- ☐ Cara the Camp Fairy
- ☐ Destiny the Rock Star Fairy
- ☐ Belle the Birthday Fairy
- ☐ Olympia the Games Fairy
- ☐ Selena the Sleepover Fairy
- ☐ Cheryl the Christmas Tree Fairy
- ☐ Florence the Friendship Fairy
- ☐ Lindsay the Luck Fairy
- ☐ Brianna the Tooth Fairy
- ☐ Autumn the Falling Leaves Fairy
- ☐ Keira the Movie Star Fairy
- ☐ Addison the April Fool's Day Fairy

■SCHOLASTIC

Find all of your favorite fairy friends at
scholastic.com/rainbowmagic

RMSPECIAL12

RAINBOW magic

These activities are magical!
Play dress-up, send friendship notes, and much more!

SCHOLASTIC
www.scholastic.com
www.rainbowmagiconline.com

HIT entertainment

RMACTIV3